FLIGHT OF THE WINGED SERPENT

Other books in the series:

DINOSAUR COVE™

FLIGHT OF THE WINGED SERPENT

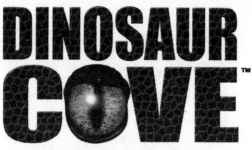

by
REX STONE

illustrated by
MIKE SPOOR

OXFORD
UNIVERSITY PRESS

Special thanks to Jan Burchett and Sara Vogler

Especially for Theo and Ben Wheadon, with love

OXFORD
UNIVERSITY PRESS

Great Clarendon Street, Oxford OX2 6DP
Oxford University Press is a department of the University of Oxford.
It furthers the University's objective of excellence in research, scholarship,
and education by publishing worldwide in

Oxford   New York

Auckland   Cape Town   Dar es Salaam   Hong Kong   Karachi
Kuala Lumpur   Madrid   Melbourne   Mexico City   Nairobi
New Delhi   Shanghai   Taipei   Toronto

With offices in

Argentina   Austria   Brazil   Chile   Czech Republic   France   Greece
Guatemala   Hungary   Italy   Japan   Poland   Portugal   Singapore
South Korea   Switzerland   Thailand   Turkey   Ukraine   Vietnam

Oxford is a registered trade mark of Oxford University Press
in the UK and in certain other countries

British Library Cataloguing in Publication Data

Data available

ISBN: 978-0-19-272095-5

1 3 5 7 9 10 8 6 4 2

Printed in Great Britain by Cox and Wyman Ltd, Reading, Berkshire

FACT FILE

➡ JAMIE HAS JUST MOVED FROM THE CITY TO LIVE IN THE LIGHTHOUSE IN DINOSAUR COVE. JAMIE'S DAD IS OPENING A DINOSAUR MUSEUM ON THE BOTTOM FLOOR OF THE LIGHTHOUSE. WHEN JAMIE GOES HUNTING FOR FOSSILS IN THE CRUMBLING CLIFFS ON THE BEACH HE MEETS A LOCAL BOY, TOM, AND THE TWO DISCOVER AN AMAZING SECRET: A WORLD WITH REAL, LIVE DINOSAURS! WALKING ON THE GROUND WITH THE DINOSAURS IS ONE THING, BUT FLYING IN THE AIR WITH THEM IS A DIFFERENT MATTER!

JAMIE

- **FULL NAME:** JAMIE MORGAN
- **AGE:** 8 YEARS
- **SIZE:** 1 JATOM*
- **TOP SPEED:** 10 KPH
- **LIKES:** FOSSIL HUNTING AND LEARNING ABOUT DINOSAURS
- **DISLIKES:** BEING STUCK INDOORS

Jamie's eye

Jamie's foot

Jamie's hand

*NOTE: A JATOM IS THE SIZE OF JAMIE OR TOM: 125 CM TALL AND 27 KG IN WEIGHT

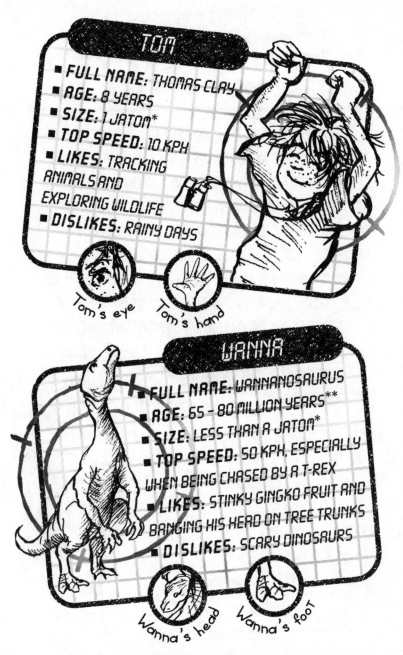

TOM

- **FULL NAME:** THOMAS CLAY
- **AGE:** 8 YEARS
- **SIZE:** 1 JATOM*
- **TOP SPEED:** 10 KPH
- **LIKES:** TRACKING ANIMALS AND EXPLORING WILDLIFE
- **DISLIKES:** RAINY DAYS

Tom's eye

Tom's hand

WANNA

- **FULL NAME:** WANNANOSAURUS
- **AGE:** 65 – 80 MILLION YEARS**
- **SIZE:** LESS THAN A JATOM*
- **TOP SPEED:** 50 KPH, ESPECIALLY WHEN BEING CHASED BY A T-REX
- **LIKES:** STINKY GINGKO FRUIT AND BANGING HIS HEAD ON TREE TRUNKS
- **DISLIKES:** SCARY DINOSAURS

Wanna's head

Wanna's foot

*NOTE: A JATOM IS THE SIZE OF JAMIE OR TOM: 125 CM TALL AND 27 KG IN WEIGHT
**NOTE: SCIENTISTS CALL THIS PERIOD THE LATE CRETACEOUS

QUETZALCOATLUS

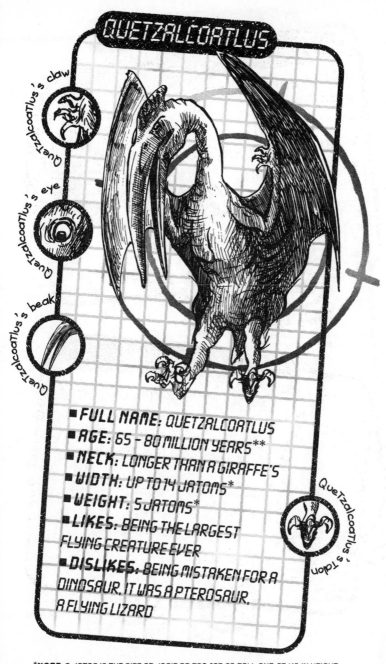

Quetzalcoatlus's claw

Quetzalcoatlus's eye

Quetzalcoatlus's beak

Quetzalcoatlus's talon

- **FULL NAME:** QUETZALCOATLUS
- **AGE:** 65 - 80 MILLION YEARS**
- **NECK:** LONGER THAN A GIRAFFE'S
- **WIDTH:** UP TO 14 JATOMS*
- **WEIGHT:** 5 JATOMS*
- **LIKES:** BEING THE LARGEST FLYING CREATURE EVER
- **DISLIKES:** BEING MISTAKEN FOR A DINOSAUR. IT WAS A PTEROSAUR. A FLYING LIZARD

*NOTE: A JATOM IS THE SIZE OF JAMIE OR TOM: 125 CM TALL AND 27 KG IN WEIGHT
**NOTE: SCIENTISTS CALL THIS PERIOD THE LATE CRETACEOUS

DINOSAUR COVE

Village

Marina

Sealight Head

Landslips where
clay and fossils are

Muddy beach

DINO CAVE

High Tide beach line

Low Tide beach line

Sea

Smuggler's Point

CHAPTER 1

'This exhibit looks so cool!' exclaimed Jamie, as his best friend Tom glued on the last miniature jungle tree.

The two boys had spent the morning painting the prehistoric landscape and were just finishing the scenery. The scale model was as big as the table top and was going to be one of the exhibits in Jamie's dad's new dinosaur museum on the bottom floor of the old lighthouse where they lived.

'The marsh is my favourite,' Tom said, putting down the glue.

The model was labelled 'Late Cretaceous Period' and had a jungle, a plain, a beach with cliffs, and an eerie-looking marsh. Dad had set up a smoke machine under the table so that smoke blew over the marsh like mist.

Dad walked into the room with the post.

'You two have done a brilliant job painting the ocean,' he told them, and grinned at their paint-splattered clothes.

'And yourselves!'

Next, Jamie and Tom added the most important items to the display—the dinosaurs! They arranged a herd of triceratops on the green plain.

'They're just right there,' said Dad. 'They look as if they're grazing.' He stuck his head into a crate and started rummaging. Sawdust flew everywhere. 'Can't find the edmontosaurus,' came his muffled voice. 'I'm sure they're in here somewhere.'

'Dad's models are great,' whispered Jamie, 'but they're not as good as the real thing.'

Jamie and Tom had a secret. They had discovered the entrance to an amazing land of living dinosaurs, and they visited it whenever they could.

Jamie picked up a Tyrannosaurus Rex and made it run across the plain towards an ankylosaurus with a roar.

Tom snatched up the ankylosaurus. 'Not such an easy meal, you bully!' He swung the tiny anky's clubbed tail at the T-Rex.

'Whoops!' Tom gasped as the T-Rex went flying out of Jamie's hand towards a shelf full of model creatures.

WHACK!

The T-Rex crashed into a large winged creature which wobbled and fell. Jamie dived like a goalie and caught it before it hit the floor.

'Good catch!' gasped Tom.

Jamie's dad came running over.

'Sorry, Mr Morgan,' said Tom. 'Is it broken?'

Jamie's dad checked the model's wings. 'No damage done,' he told them. 'Now, where should this go on the display?'

Jamie looked at the long beak, the outstretched wings, and bony crest on the head. 'It's a sort of pterosaur, isn't it?'

'Yes, it's a quetzalcoatlus. Here's its label.'

'*Ket-sal-kow-at-lus*,' Jamie read. 'That's a mouthful.'

'The biggest flying reptile of them all,' Dad explained. 'It had a twelve metre wingspan.'

'That's more than six Dads lying head to toe.' Jamie flung his arms out wide.

'What a monster!' Tom said.

'One thing we don't know

is where these quetzies nested,' said Dad.
'On the marsh, on the beach, or in the
jungle.' He put the quetzy back on the shelf.
'Here's a quest for you, boys. Do some
research and help me decide where on the
model to put it. That'll keep you out of
trouble.'

Jamie and Tom grinned at each other.
They knew exactly where to find out where
the quetzalcoatlus nested—Dino World!

Jamie scooped up his backpack and charged
after Tom down the rocky steps from the
lighthouse. They raced across the
pebbly beach, whooping with
excitement, to the steep
headland path. Clambering
over the mossy boulders they were
soon at the old smugglers' cave—and the
entrance to their secret world.

Tom slipped inside with Jamie close behind. They squeezed through the tiny opening to the second chamber. Jamie shone his torch over the rock floor.

'Here are the footprints,' he said. 'Let's go!'

One step at a time, Jamie and Tom followed the fossilized dinosaur tracks that led to the wall at the back of the cave. One . . . two . . . The familiar crack of light appeared in the wall . . . three . . . four . . . The crack widened . . . Five!

When Jamie opened his eyes, the ground was spongy under his feet. Jamie and Tom were in Dino World again!

CHAPTER 2

Jamie stepped out of the cave and squinted in the bright sunlight. He breathed in the hot, damp air. 'Awesome!'

A bristly tongue licked his hand. A little dinosaur with greenish brown markings stood looking up hopefully at him.

'It's Wanna!' he cried.

Tom gave the wannanosaurus a welcoming pat on his hard, flat head. Wanna wagged his tail happily and stuck out his tongue to investigate a blue spot on Jamie's shorts.

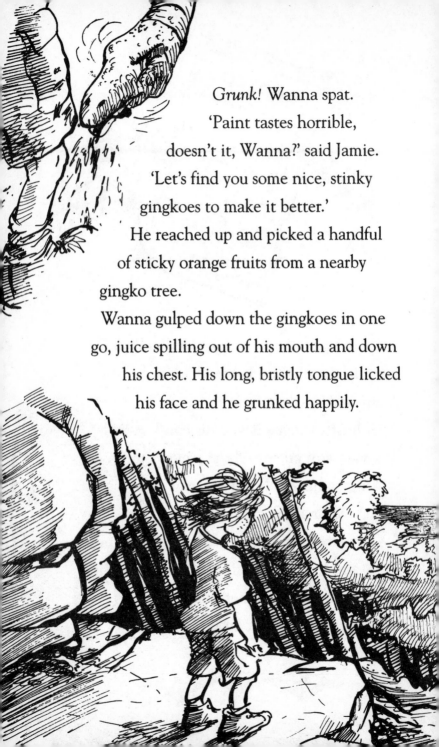

Grunk! Wanna spat.
'Paint tastes horrible,
doesn't it, Wanna?' said Jamie.
'Let's find you some nice, stinky
gingkoes to make it better.'
He reached up and picked a handful
of sticky orange fruits from a nearby
gingko tree.
Wanna gulped down the gingkoes in one
go, juice spilling out of his mouth and down
his chest. His long, bristly tongue licked
his face and he grunked happily.

Jamie stuck a few more gingkoes in his backpack.

The boys went to the edge of the steep slope that led down to the jungle. They scanned the thick green canopy of trees below.

'One thing's for sure,' said Tom, 'quetzies couldn't live in there—not with that huge wingspan. The trees are too close together. And I don't see any nests in the tree tops.'

Jamie opened his Fossil Finder and put quetzalcoatlus in the search.

'*THOUGHT TO HAVE EATEN LIKE HERON, DIVING DOWN FOR FISH,*' he read. 'So maybe they live near water.'

'Misty Lagoon?' said Tom. 'But I only remember seeing smaller pterosaurs there—nothing as big as a quetzy.'

'How about White Ocean?' said Jamie eagerly. He shielded his eyes with his hand and peered out over the jungle, to where the ocean waves broke in a white line.

Tom whipped his compass out of his pocket. 'West it is.'

The boys made their way down into the thick, damp undergrowth of the jungle. Wanna ran happily alongside them. He stopped to headbutt a pine tree and greedily ate the cones that fell. The shower of cones disturbed a host of brightly coloured butterflies as

big as the boys' hands.
They swarmed for a moment
and then settled on a bush
covered in white flowers.

The boys crossed the
river and gradually the dense
jungle thinned. They passed
the lagoon and the ground
became sandy, with tall, spiky
plants shooting up in places.

'I can hear waves breaking,'
exclaimed Tom. 'Race you!'

They charged through the last few
trees and out into the sunlight.

'Wow!' breathed Jamie, skidding to
a halt. He pointed down the beach.
'Check out those cliffs. They're even
higher than back in Dinosaur Cove.'

Sharp ledges and leafy green bushes
covered the huge cliff-face. In front of

them, the golden beach stretched towards the water. Wanna sniffed around, getting his snout covered in sand.

'Maybe this is his first trip to the seaside.' Jamie laughed. 'Sorry we forgot the bucket and spade, Wanna.'

'Awesome!' shouted Tom above the sound of the crashing breakers and the gusting wind. 'Look at those waves. Fantastic for surfing.'

'If you don't mind the predators,' Jamie

reminded him. 'I bet it's not just lobsters and crabs under there.' He typed *LATE CRETACEOUS SEA CREATURES* into the Fossil Finder and scrolled down the entries. *'ELASMOSAURUS: HUGE, LONG-NECKED, MARINE REPTILE.*

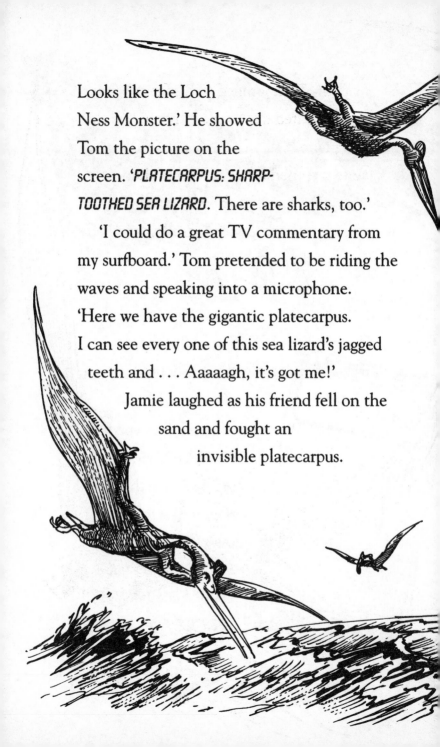

Looks like the Loch
Ness Monster.' He showed
Tom the picture on the
screen. '*PLATECARPUS: SHARP-
TOOTHED SEA LIZARD*. There are sharks, too.'

'I could do a great TV commentary from
my surfboard.' Tom pretended to be riding the
waves and speaking into a microphone.
'Here we have the gigantic platecarpus.
I can see every one of this sea lizard's jagged
teeth and . . . Aaaaagh, it's got me!'

Jamie laughed as his friend fell on the
sand and fought an
invisible platecarpus.

Suddenly Tom jumped to his feet. 'What's that?' He pointed out to the horizon. 'It's the size of a plane.'

Jamie screened his eyes with his hand. Far away over the sea, a huge winged creature was gliding in large graceful circles, rising and falling with the air currents.

Tom whistled. 'It's just like your dad's model. And look, here come some more.'

The two boys looked at each other.

'It's a quetzalcoatlus!' they shouted.

CHAPTER 3

Jamie and Tom watched as the huge quetzies
made lazy circles above the surf. One of them
was getting closer.

'It's searching for fish,' said Tom. 'Do you
think its nest is nearby?'

'It might be in the sand,' suggested Jamie.
'Like a turtle's.'

They walked along the high tide line,
crunching through fragments of patterned
baculite shell, but couldn't see any imprints or
patterns in the ground to suggest a nest.

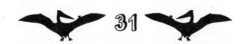

31

'Wouldn't this look good in your dad's museum?' Tom said, picking up a shell. 'Shame it would just turn to dust if we took it back.'

'Even if we could,' added Jamie, 'these have been extinct for millions of years. Dad would want to know how we found one that's not a fossil.'

Wanna trotted down the beach and looked suspiciously at the waves.

'Going for a paddle, Wanna?' called Tom.

The little dinosaur crept towards the edge of the water and stuck in his snout.

Grunk!

He spluttered and darted back. The boys burst out laughing.

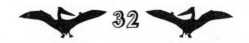

'The salt must taste worse
than paint,' said Jamie.
'Poor Wanna.'

Wanna scratched at his mouth
with his front claws as if he was trying to get
rid of the taste.

Then Tom spotted a cave at the bottom
of the cliffs. 'That would be a great hiding
place for the quetzy's nest.'

The boys went to investigate. Jamie pulled
out his torch and shone it into the dark
beyond the cave entrance but it was empty.
There was no sign of a quetzy nest.

AAAARK!

The boys whirled round at the deafening

sound behind them. An enormous shadow was moving over the sand. They dived into the cave mouth. Wanna grunked in alarm and followed.

A gigantic creature swept down and landed on the sand with a loud flapping of wings that sounded like boat sails in the wind. Jamie and Tom stared in amazement. In front of them were two long scaly legs with massive clawed feet. As they looked up they could see a featherless body and neck that seemed to snake up to the sky. It stood above them, as tall as a house, twisting its long neck slowly this way and that. Then it opened its beak and gave out a loud *AAAARK!*

'It's the quetzy,' breathed Tom.

'That's one weird reptile,' said Jamie in amazement. 'Like a fold-up paper aeroplane with skin for wings.'

The huge pterosaur began to clump awkwardly across the sand, head forward,

using the claws on its wings as front feet.

'Bats walk like that,' said Tom. 'I've seen it on a wildlife programme.'

A gust of wind buffeted the quetzy. It ran a few steps on its long skinny legs, caught the updraught and took off.

'See where it goes!' cried Jamie.

The boys dashed out from the shelter of the cave mouth and watched the quetzalcoatlus rise. The wind buffeted it back towards the cliffs, but soon it turned and soared, flapping its powerful wings to gain height. It circled around the cliff top and descended, feet out for landing. At last, with a loud *AAARK*, it disappeared from view.

'I bet its nest is up *there*,' said Jamie. 'We have to get to the top.'

'It'll be a tough climb,' said Tom, squinting up at the cliff-face. 'But we can do it. There are indents for our feet.'

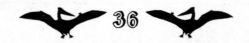

'And we can use
the bushes to cling to,'
agreed Jamie.

SQUAWK!

Something landed on
the sand behind them.
It lay on its back with its
skinny feet in the air.
It looked like a large,
featherless chicken.

'Where did that come
from?' exclaimed Tom,
staring up at the cliffs.

'I don't know,' gasped Jamie.
'Watch out!'

They darted back as a
second one fell out of the sky
and plopped down on to the
sand. 'They must be coming from
up there,' Tom said.

A third creature appeared over
the top of the cliffs. It flapped its
wings desperately and then cartwheeled
down, squawking, to land right in front
of them.

'They've got crests.' Tom pointed to the
little bony lump on top of each head. 'Long
beaks, claws on their wings . . . '

'They're baby quetzies!'

The boys watched as the three young
reptiles struggled to their feet and waddled up
and down flapping their wings.

'They're trying to take off,' said Tom.

'They look like big wind-up toys.' Jamie
grinned at the funny sight.

Grunk, grunk!

Wanna scuttled up to the gawky creatures.
The baby quetzies peered down at him and
squawked happily. 'What is it, boy?' asked
Jamie. 'Are you saying hello?'

Grunk!

Wanna nudged the nearest chick with his nose, then darted out of reach. The little quetzies clumped after him on all fours, squeaking with delight. Wanna stopped, waggled his tail at them and dashed off down the beach. His new playmates followed.

Tom chuckled. 'They're playing tag. Let's get a closer look.'

As soon as they saw the boys coming, the baby quetzies left Wanna and waddled towards them.

'They're not scared of us,' said Tom. 'They look really friendly.'

'Whoa!' Jamie backed off as a long pointed beak was pushed in his face, and another pecked at his trainers. 'A bit too friendly.'

AARK! The boys looked up. The mother quetzy was gliding in circles, looking down angrily, blocking out the sun.

'Run!' shouted Jamie.

Jamie and Tom flattened themselves against the cliff-face, but Wanna hadn't noticed the danger. He ran round the babies, grunking and nudging them to play again.

'Wanna's in danger,' said Tom. 'The mother might attack him!'

'Come here, Wanna,' Jamie shouted but the little quetzies were making so much noise that Wanna didn't hear him.

AAARK!

The huge quetzalcoatlus began to descend,
stretching out long, sharp claws as she came.

'We've got to save Wanna!' yelled Jamie,
darting forwards.

'It's too late.' Tom pulled his friend back.
'There's nothing we can do.'

Swoosh! The boys felt the rush of air as
the giant pterosaur swooped down over the
sand. A second later she was making for the sky.

The babies were gone—and so was Wanna!

Jamie and Tom stared open-mouthed as the quetzalcoatlus rose in the air. Wanna and the three chicks were dangling from her claws. They could see the little dinosaur's tail waggling with fright.

Jamie shook Tom's arm. 'We've got to get up those cliffs,' he urged. 'We must rescue Wanna.'

'Too right,' said Tom. 'Before he's turned into quetzy food!'

They began to climb, side by side. It was a slow job. The cliff footholds were very small

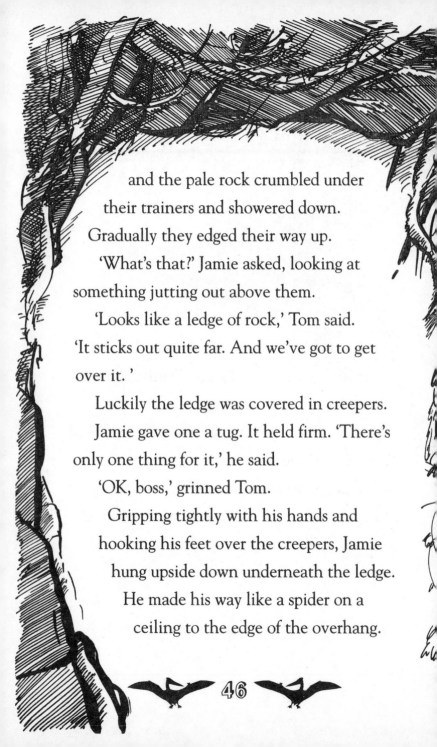

and the pale rock crumbled under
their trainers and showered down.
Gradually they edged their way up.

'What's that?' Jamie asked, looking at
something jutting out above them.

'Looks like a ledge of rock,' Tom said.
'It sticks out quite far. And we've got to get
over it.'

Luckily the ledge was covered in creepers.

Jamie gave one a tug. It held firm. 'There's
only one thing for it,' he said.

'OK, boss,' grinned Tom.

Gripping tightly with his hands and
hooking his feet over the creepers, Jamie
hung upside down underneath the ledge.
He made his way like a spider on a
ceiling to the edge of the overhang.

He scrabbled with his
fingers to find a handhold
on the top of the ledge.

Suddenly he lost his
grip and found himself
hanging by his trainers.
It was like dangling from
a giant climbing frame—a
climbing frame with a
deadly drop beneath it.

'Jamie!' yelled Tom
in alarm.

'I'm OK,' Jamie shouted
back. He swung his arms up as hard as he
could and on the third attempt managed to
grab the foliage again. He waited until he'd
got his breath back, then, tensing every
muscle, he heaved himself onto the top of
the ledge.

Soon Tom's hand appeared. Jamie took

him firmly by the wrist and helped him up. The boys saw that the top of the ledge was also covered by a spongy bed of creepers.

'Awesome!' breathed Tom. 'We did it.'

'And there's the top of the cliffs,' cried Jamie, pointing a little way above their heads. 'Wanna, here we come!'

They scrambled up to the cliff edge and looked over. It was nothing like the cliffs back home, which were covered in grass and wild flowers. Here there was bare rock with a few scattered prickly plants sticking up.

The mother quetzy sat a little way from them.

'There's no sign of Wanna,' said Jamie,
'or the babies.'

'Let's get behind that bush with the red
flowers,' whispered Tom. 'The quetzy
won't be able to see us there.'

Jamie and Tom crawled
commando style to the thick
bush. Jamie carefully parted some
leaves. The mother quetzy filled
his view.

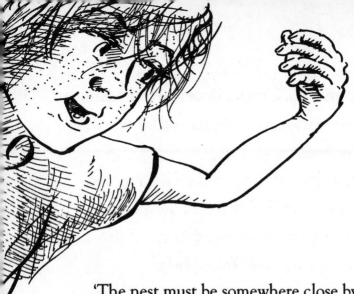

'The nest must be somewhere close by,'
he told Tom. 'But it's hard to spot it with that
huge pterosaur in the way.'

'Ask her to move,' grinned Tom.

'*You* ask her!'

As if she had heard, the mother quetzy
waddled to the cliff edge, folded its wings and
raised its head, gazing out to sea.

'Look at the three bony crests over there,'
whispered Jamie. 'Those are the babies. The
mother must be guarding them in their nest.'

The baby quetzies were sitting in a hollow
a few metres away.

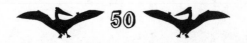

'But where's Wanna?' Tom grabbed Jamie's arm. 'What if we're too late and they've already had him for dinner?'

Grunk, grunk!

A cone-shaped leathery hat with two brown eyes under it appeared over the edge of the nest.

'There he is!' exclaimed Tom.

'He's OK,' breathed Jamie in relief. 'But what's he wearing?'

'It's one of the quetzy eggshells,' Tom giggled. He stuck a hand out of the bush. 'Here, Wanna,' he beckoned.

'Come on, Wanna,' Jamie tried to coax him.

But Wanna just stared at them. He seemed comfortable with his new friends.

'How do we lure him out?' said Tom.

Jamie rummaged in his backpack. 'I'll offer him a gingko. That should bring him running.'

Trying to keep out of sight of the mother, Jamie crawled towards the nest. He had reached the edge when she spotted him.

AAARK!
Jamie ducked as
the huge wing nearly
caught him. He darted
back to the bushes and Tom
pulled him between the leaves and out of
sight. The gingko was squashed in his hand.

'It's just like on the documentaries,' said
Tom. 'The mother is protecting her young
and that makes her very dangerous.'

'One whack and I'd have been over the
edge,' puffed Jamie. 'Now what?'

Tom didn't answer. He was looking up.

Another quetzy was circling the nest.

'That one's even bigger than this one,' he said. 'It could be the dad.'

AARK, AAARK!

The male quetzy landed next to the nest. His cry was deep and rumbling. The babies greeted him with screeches and squeals. Their heads bobbed and they eagerly opened their beaks. Wanna sat looking puzzled under his leathery hat. The dad bent his head down in a sudden motion and opened his mouth wide— right over Wanna's head. The boys heard a strange gurgling noise from his throat.

'He's going to eat him!' Jamie gasped. 'We've got to do something.'

But the male quetzy moved his head away from Wanna and over one of his babies. He made the strange gurgling sound again and suddenly was sick into the baby quetzy's

open beak. The little chick gulped hungrily.
Then the dad bent to the next chick and
puked again. The chick opened its mouth,
caught the goo and gulped hungrily.

'Gross!' said Jamie.

'It's just like birds feeding their young,' said
Tom. 'They mash down the food in their own
throats and then bring it back up for them.
And it's Wanna's turn now.'

The father gurgled again and all at once
Wanna and his eggshell hat were covered in
steaming yellow goo. Wanna looked surprised.

Jamie laughed. 'They think he's one of
their chicks!'

CHAPTER 5

SEARCH

Wanna shook his head, splattering yellow goo
everywhere. His eggshell hat went flying.
Then he clambered out of the nest and began
to sniff and scuff at the ground.

'That's our Wanna,' whispered Tom.
'He never sits still for long. He's too nosy.'

'I'd get out if a dinosaur was sick on my
head,' said Jamie.

Tom craned round the bush. 'Wanna,'
he called softly. 'Here, boy.'

AAARK!

The mother quetzy had seen
Wanna. Wriggling her wings
irritably, she scuttled round the
nest and nudged him back
with her beak.

When the father had finished feeding all
the chicks, he took off and soared away.

'This is our best chance to get Wanna,'
said Jamie. 'I'd rather face one fierce quetzy
than two.'

'Agreed,' Tom nodded.

The chicks began to squawk excitedly as
the mother picked one of them up in her beak
and plonked it down at the cliff edge.

'What's she doing?' Jamie gasped.
'The baby's going to fall off again.'

The little quetzy
teetered on the edge
for a moment and
suddenly leapt off.
They just had time
to see it flapping its
wings frantically before it
plummeted out of sight.
The mother didn't seem
to mind. She nudged
another chick out of the
nest and pushed it to
the drop. This one
flapped its wings and
actually flew for a few
seconds before it
plunged down.
They could hear
its happy squawks
as it fell.

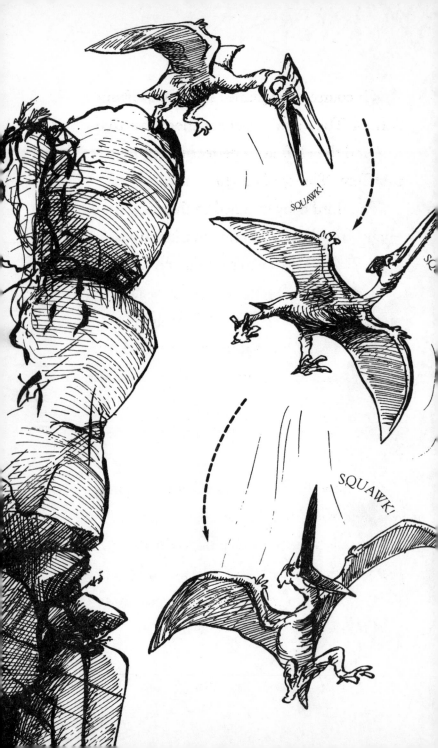

'Of course,' said Jamie. 'It's Quetzy Flying School. The mum's teaching them how to fly.'

'And the cliffs are a perfect launching site,' said Tom. 'Plenty of height.'

The third baby waddled to the edge, opened its wings wide and vanished from sight. The boys heard a squeal of triumph and the little quetzy reappeared, flapping its wings and squawking at its mother. The mum squawked back encouragingly. Then the baby flew in a large circle and headed off out to sea.

'Perhaps the mother will go off after them and we can rescue Wanna,' said Tom hopefully.

But now the mother quetzy was nudging Wanna towards the edge.

Jamie looked from Wanna to the cliff top. 'She wants him to fly too!'

'Uh oh,' Tom said. 'We've got to save him!'

63

They darted out from their hiding place.
Wanna was squatting on the edge of the cliff.
He grunked and flapped his front legs as if he
had been watching the others.

AARK! The mother quetzy was getting
impatient. She prodded Wanna and he nearly
fell off the cliff.

Suddenly Jamie knew what to do.

'Grab him!' he yelled to Tom. 'We'll all
jump down and aim for the ledge below.
It's our only chance.'

Dodging under the mother quetzy's wings,
the boys charged at Wanna, seized him round
the middle and leapt off the cliff.

CHAPTER 6

Crunch!

They landed in a heap in the bouncy creepers. One of the babies was there and it squealed with delight when it saw Wanna appear in front of him. The boys gave each other a high five.

'We made it!'

AAARK!

'It's the mum,' said Jamie urgently, looking up.

The quetzy was peering
over the edge of the cliff.
She poked her long beak
down and the boys had to
roll out of the way. She
opened her wings and
took to the air. 'We'd
better get out of here
before she circles round
to rescue her chick—
and Wanna. But how
are we going to get him
to the beach?'

'Perhaps we can
make a rope out of the
creepers,' suggested Tom.

'Then we can lower him.'

'It would work as long as we tie good knots,' said Jamie.

Grunk, grunk!

They turned to see Wanna clambering to the far end of the ledge and disappearing from view.

'Wait, Wanna,' cried Tom, scrambling across to see where he'd gone. 'You'll fall!'

But to his surprise Wanna was trotting happily across the cliff face. He'd found a little trail that wound right down to the sand. The boys followed, placing each foot carefully on the narrow path.

'This is easier than the climb up,' said Tom.

'But not as exciting,' replied Jamie.

Swoosh! The mother quetzy swooped up past them, claws outstretched.

'She's come for her baby,' said Tom. 'I hope.'

The quetzy glided gracefully to the ledge

and soon had her chick in her grasp. She
made a wide, slow circle over the beach.
The boys held their breath.

Was she coming for Wanna now?

But after an anxious moment she rose to
the cliff top and disappeared.

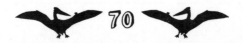

70

As soon as the boys stepped onto the sand, Wanna bounded up and head butted them affectionately.

'Let's get you home, boy,' said Tom. 'Before your new mother comes looking for you.'

They set off back into the jungle, Wanna running alongside them, grunking happily.

As they followed the river back to Wanna's cave, Jamie stopped and wrinkled his nose. 'What's that smell?'

'It's Wanna,' Tom laughed. 'He's still covered in quetzy puke.'

'Yuck!' Jamie held his nose. 'Someone needs a bath.'

He waded into the shallows and held out a gingko. Wanna bounded into the river.

'Great,' said Tom, jumping in to join them. 'We can give him a shower.'

He cupped his hands in the water and splashed Wanna all over.

Then Wanna turned and thumped the surface with his tail. Jamie and Tom got soaked.

'Thanks, Wanna,' said Tom. 'At least that gross yellow puke has gone.'

Finally, they climbed out of the shadows and made their way up the hill to Wanna's cave.

Grunk.

Wanna ran straight to his nest and curled up.

'You've got the right nest this time,' grinned Jamie. He took the last gingkoes out of his bag and put them by Wanna's side. 'See you soon, little friend.'

They put their feet in the dinosaur footprints and walked backwards towards the cave wall into the smugglers' cave. They hurried out of the cave and down the headland, running all the way along the beach to the path that led up Sealight Head. After waiting a little while for the sun to dry out their clothes, they raced up the steps, two at a time, and burst through the door of the lighthouse.

'We must have been away ages,' gasped Jamie. 'Dad's done so much.'

They gazed at the breathtaking displays of dinosaur models and fossils all around the room.

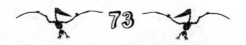

'Awesome!' Tom pointed at a huge ammonite. 'It's as big as a tyre.'

Jamie wandered round, taking it all in. 'The triceratops skull looks great up on the wall.'

His dad came in at that moment, laden with books.

'Hello there, boys,' he called. 'Found anything out about the quetzy nest?'

The boys went over to the model Cretaceous landscape. 'We think it would have nested here on the cliff top,' said Jamie. 'There's lots of room for those huge wings and it's a perfect take-off point.'

'The babies could learn to fly from there,'
added Tom eagerly. 'It's very high and there'd
be uplift from the wind coming off the ocean.'

'Good thinking, boys,' said Jamie's dad.
He placed the quetzalcoatlus carefully down
on the cliff top. 'They'd be able to skim down
over the sea and catch their dinner.'

Jamie looked at the quetzalcoatlus
model, its wings outstretched ready for flight.
He winked at Tom.

'That's not all they catch,' he whispered.

DINOSAUR WORLD

- - - - - BOYS' ROUTE

Ju

Misty
Lagoon

White
Ocean

Far Away Mountains

Crashing Rock Falls

Great Plains

Fang Rock

Gingko Hill

GLOSSARY

Baculite (back-you-lite) – an extinct sea creature that swam upside down with its head sticking out from the bottom of its long thin shell. Because baculite fossils are fragile, fossil hunters rarely find a fossilized baculite shell intact.

Elasmosaurus (ee-laz-mow-sor-us) – a long-necked prehistoric sea creature with a small head, sharp teeth and four flippers. Elasmosaurus may have stretched 14 metres long, with its neck making up half of its total length.

Gingko (gink-oh) – a tree native to China called a 'living fossil' because fossils of it have been found dating back millions of years, yet they are still around today. Also known as the stink bomb tree because of its smelly apricot-like fruit.

Platecarpus (plat-ee-carp-us) – an extinct sharp-toothed lizard with a long, flat tail and flippers which may have swum like a snake in prehistoric waters.

Pterosaur (ter-oh-sor) – a prehistoric flying reptile. Its wings were leathery and light and some of these 'winged lizards' had fur on their bodies and bony crests on their heads.

Quetzalcoatlus (ket-sal-kow-at-lus) – one of the largest flying animals ever. Named after the Aztec feathered serpent god Quetzalcoatl, this prehistoric bird had a long neck, toothless jaw and a long bony crest on top of its head. Its clawed wings could span up to 15 metres across.

Wannanosaurus (wah-nan-oh-sor-us) – a dinosaur that only ate plants and used its hard, flat skull to defend itself. Named after the place it was discovered: Wannano in China.

If you blink you'll miss me...
and I'm coming next!